SNAZZY
CAT CAPERS

MEOW or NEVER

For Sam, Max, Zach, Jake, Jackson, Ethan, Ella, Anna,
Colton, Charlotte, Claire, Dean, Mackenzie, Parker, Tanner,
Finn, Kristie, Mike, Rich, Kerri, Kim, Rob, our parents &
parental types, friends, librarians, and everyone who believes
that the world is infinitely snazzier with teamwork.

[Imprint]
MAKE YOUR MARK

A part of Macmillan Publishing Group, LLC
120 Broadway, New York, NY 10271

SNAZZY CAT CAPERS: MEOW OR NEVER. Copyright
© 2020 by GrumpyFish Creative, Inc. All rights reserved.
Printed in the United States of America by
LSC Communications, Harrisonburg, Virginia.

Library of Congress Control Number: 2020908625

ISBN 978-1-250-14349-5 (hardcover) / ISBN 978-1-250-14348-8 (ebook)

Our books may be purchased in bulk for promotional, educational, or business use. Please
contact your local bookseller or the Macmillan Corporate and Premium Sales Department at
(800) 221-7945 ext. 5442 or by email at MacmillanSpecialMarkets@macmillan.com.

Book design by Eileen Savage

Illustrations by Neil Hooson

Imprint logo designed by Amanda Spielman

First edition, 2020

1 3 5 7 9 10 8 6 4 2

mackids.com

Attention, cat burglars: The Furry Feline Burglary Institute (FFBI) officially deems
book thievery dishonorable. Comply or be fur-ever cursed with puddles and poodles.

SNAZZY
CAT CAPERS

MEOW or NEVER

DEANNA KENT　　　**ILLUSTRATED BY NEIL HOOSON**

{Imprint}
MAKE YOUR MARK
NEW YORK

FUR-WORD

JUST WHO IS OPHELIA VON HAIRBALL V OF BURGLARIA?

MSN Mews says she'll "outclass the classiest with her fur-bulous cat burglar moves and infamous heists!" If you follow her capers, you'll probably notice her amazing costumes, gadgets, and gear—especially her unique cat burglar suit and one-of-a-kind Personal Ultra Gadget robo-dog, P.U.G. Not that I'm fishing for compliments, but I designed those. I'm Ophelia's personal fin-ventor, assigned by the Furry Feline Burglary Institute (FFBI). Ophelia still thinks she works better solo, but I've saved her fluffy white tail more than once. It's my dream that she will soon invite me along on all her outrageous shenanigans.

—*Oscar F. Gold (Inventor #17)*

"The best castles are like the best cupcakes, gifts, and cats—fancy on the outside and filled with surprises."

—Ophelia von Hairball V

1

SWEET, SWEET PLANS

With the wind in her face, she felt like a bright, shiny supernova. The air from the whirring helicopter blade puffed her tail into a big white cloud. A well-disguised Ophelia waved at her welcoming committee. Of course, the crowd had no idea they had just let an infamous cat burglar on the red-carpeted rooftop of their snazzy Swiss castle.

Ophelia held tight to her jewel-encrusted hat until the wind from the chopper died down. Cameras flashed and photographers ooohed and aaahed. Her poses for the press were purr-fect.

"Welcome!" her host gushed. "We're so honored to have you at the Swiss Hiss Confection Castle! Each and every one of our world-famous treats are made right here. I'm Ruby, great-great-great-granddaughter of the company's founder. It's a pleasure to meet you, Ali. I'll be showing you around."

Comfortable in her disguise, Ophelia grinned and politely held out a paw. She always enjoyed good old-fashioned manners.

"It's very nice to meet you, too," she stated simply.

"Nobody can believe the one and only Ali Kat Cooke, world-famous food critic, is visiting to test our world-class cakes! We're very grateful your agent contacted us. We just can't wait to hear what you think of our newest recipe!" Ruby grinned. "Our chefs have been perfecting it for years. We hope you adore it."

Ophelia mewed back slyly. Of course, Ophelia von Hairball V of Burglaria *wasn't* a food critic at all. Although she liked the finer things in life—including very good cake—the world's number one cat burglar didn't normally have time to travel around the globe and write about it. So while it was true Ophelia was excited to try the newest treat that the Swiss Hiss Confectionery Company had created, her reason for being at the castle was *actually* to nab the top-secret recipe and take it back to her lair.

Ophelia von Hairball V planned to use the best cake recipe in the world to make a dessert masterpiece—a special nine-layer catnip birthday cake for MEW, the director of the Furry Feline Burglary Institute. Since MEW had everything (and could easily take whatever she didn't have), Ophelia wanted to make her something special—a cake crafted entirely from scratch. It would be the most delicious gift *ever*. Most important, it would beat any tacky present Ophelia's (very mean) cousin Pierre would buy MEW. It was critical that Ophelia give MEW a better gift than Pierre—their rivalry was epic.

Ophelia followed Ruby away from the

helicopter. They soon approached the large glass door on the castle's rooftop. Ophelia peered at herself and admired her stellar disguise. It was one she'd put together herself.

It hadn't been hard to create a look for Ali Kat Cooke because the famous food critic had *never before been photographed*! Ali kept her identity secret for a good reason: She always pretended to be a regular patron at the restaurants she visited so she could judge food anonymously. If nobody knew who she was, nobody would give her special treatment.

Ali's column ran on all the major news sites and was read by millions all over the globe. If a restaurant was given a good review by Ali Kat Cooke, it meant *instant* success.

Inside the castle, Ophelia walked down a long, gleaming marble corridor to a central spiral staircase. Beside her, Ruby buzzed with excitement. "Did you know that in the entire hiss-tory of the Swiss Hiss empire, nobody has ever been invited to see the inner workings of the palace? Until you, that is."

"Well, I'm thrilled to be here, Ruby." Ophelia was sincere. "And may I just say you've got the very best name in the whole entire world? I do love rubies."

Her host beamed.

Normally, Ophelia's heists involved gleaming gems and priceless jewels—not recipes. But because she was an agent for the FFBI, her cat burglary prowess wasn't so much about taking something but more about proving she *could* take something.

With a firm belief in time-honored traditions, Ophelia had been the FFBI's top cat burglar for years. With class, pizzazz, and a whole lot of snazz, she'd stolen precious jewelry, one-of-a-kind motor-cycles, and even a dangerous ancient device. But it wasn't always easy. Ophelia had to be at the top of her game because her ne-fur-ious cousin Pierre (the FFBI's number *two* cat burglar) was always chasing her tail for the number one spot.

Ophelia and Pierre had been rivals since child-hood. Except for their similar fierce competitive streaks, they were complete opposites. Ophelia fol-lowed the rules, and Pierre cheated every chance he could. Ophelia was meticulous, and Pierre was sloppy. Worst of all, when they were teensy fluff-ball kittens, Pierre had stolen Ophelia's special action figure, Captain Claw-some—which had been a gift from their grandmother. (Ophelia was determined to get it back—sooner rather than later!)

They approached a spiral staircase. Ophelia could see a fancy kitchen on the floor below. But as they neared the stairs, a wall of security guards stopped them. Ruby looked at Ophelia sheepishly. "I hope you don't mind. There's so much security. We do, after all, hold the one and only recipe for the best and most celebrated cake in the world. They'll need to see your passport."

"But of course." Ophelia nodded. She reached into her handbag and pulled out a passport. "Here I am. International food critic *Ali Kat Cooke*."

The head guard examined the document closely. Ophelia wasn't worried about the guard's scrutiny. Ophelia's disguises and forgeries were always purr-fectly executed. She went the extra mile. He nodded and passed it back to her.

"We've become more strict lately," Ruby confessed. "There were rumors of people hunting around online for this castle's blueprints."

Ophelia managed to look shocked, even though it was probably her snooping that had set alarm bells off. (Her acting skills often came in handy during heists.) "Wow!" she said. "Are we in danger of being robbed?"

"Oh, no! Please don't worry," Ruby assured her with a whisper. "I'm not supposed to say, but we've really bumped up security precautions. The blueprints online are *all wrong*. On the advice of our chief security officer, we redesigned the entire castle's interior to deter thieves! We never released the new plans!"

Ophelia hissed under her breath.

"Never hand over your dreams, your favorite
shoes, or your cake recipe."

—Ophelia von Hairball V

2

UN-FUR-GETTABLE SIDEKICK

Without a solid plan, Ophelia needed to buy some time. A few feet from where they stood, she saw a grand hallway. The Swiss Hiss family photos lined the walls. "Ruby, before we go down to the kitchen, do you mind if I take a moment to look around up here? I adore hiss-tory, and I'd like to include some of your family stories in my *glowing* review."

"But of course!" Ruby was proud. "Take your time!"

Once Ophelia was out of Ruby's earshot, she dialed her fishy inventor. Oscar F. Gold immediately answered the video call.

Ophelia was suspicious. Oscar was *always* over-eager to be part of any adventure. "You don't seem too busy. You answered on the first ring."

"Let me show you!" the fish told her with gusto. Oscar turned his phone to show her where he was. "Look at my gorgeous surroundings! P.U.G. and I are very much enjoying a ski hill." Ophelia could see the fish and their Personal Ultra Gadget on top of a snowy mountain.

Oscar had engineered P.U.G., a robotic invention, to look an awful lot like their annoying next-door neighbor—a dog called Thug, who was a member of the FFBI's rival organization, the Central Canine Intelligence Agency, or CCIA. She didn't like Thug, and she didn't like P.U.G. And it was a bit annoying that Oscar had created it.

When the FFBI first assigned Oscar to Ophelia, she hadn't wanted an inventor at all. The fish was nice enough and plenty smart, but she'd always preferred to work alone. However, on several recent heists, Oscar had been very helpful. Slowly, Ophelia had warmed up to the idea of having him around *once* in a while. (Though she hadn't invited him to Switzerland.)

Oscar moved his phone cam around more. "See? *We're so busy,*" he stated. "And very much enjoying a few moguls while we test out my latest jet-propulsion gadget."

"Love your ski outfit," she commented. As well as devising great gadgets and gear, Oscar designed stellar costumes and disguises.

"Thank you." He beamed. Although Ophelia was sometimes difficult to work with, he had been a devoted fan-fish since the first time he'd heard stories about her.

"Hold on, Oscar." Ophelia caught a glimpse of something oddly fur-miliar in Oscar's background. "Where are you?" Ophelia asked suspiciously. "Big White? Niseko? Telluride?"

"Um ... we're on a really snowy hill."

"Yes. In which country?"

"Well, er—Switzerland," Oscar replied sheepishly.

"Switzerland?" Ophelia grinned. "Well, well. Isn't that just a *huge*, fishy coincidence," she replied. "As you know, I'm here in Switzerland, too!"

"Oh. Er—uh, that's odd we ended up in the same country."

Down the hall, Ophelia saw Ruby check her watch. Ophelia pretended to take pictures of the photographs on the wall as she whispered to Oscar.

LISTEN, OSCAR. I NEED YOU—

"You need me?" He sounded thrilled. "Ophelia, *did you just say you need me?*"

Ophelia felt her fur start to stand up. "Oscar—I do need you . . . to look something up for me."

"You can't take it back now! Ophelia, I'm your

loyal sidekick, and I will be there by your side in sixty seconds flat!"

"What do you mean, sixty seconds?"

"Well, uh, the hill we're at is super close to where you are."

"HOW CLOSE?"

"Look out the window. . . ."

Ophelia sighed. "I actually just need some recon. Some information! I'm—"

"I know what you're doing," Oscar said. "You're

in the Swiss Hiss Confection Castle looking for the super-secret cake recipe." He'd done his research. "Let me guess: You've probably already made it past the first set of guards, and some enthusiastic employee let it slip that the blueprints you memorized are outdated. So now you need my help finding the new building plans. Am I right?"

Growl. The cat burglar didn't want to admit he was 100 percent right. But she didn't have time to wait for her greatest fan-fish to offer a helping fin.

"I presume you are wearing your cat burglar costume under that fancy disguise?"

Ophelia grinned into the phone. "I am."

"Brilliant!" Oscar had designed the cat burglar outfit and was proud of all its features. "First, put your earpiece in so I can talk to you without anyone getting suspicious. Then push the gold button on your left paw."

Ophelia put the earpiece in but knew better than to push *any* of Oscar's gold buttons without first asking what it might do. "I'll need more intel about that gold button," she said. "And hurry, please. I'm running out of time here."

"There's only one of mew, and you're the cat's meow. Never forget it."

—Ophelia von Hairball V

3

WIZARD OF PAWS!

The gold button on your left paw will deploy a small drone that looks like an insect. It's programmed to survey the building and transmit everything it sees. You'll have a 3-D hologram of the building within seconds."

He might've been slightly annoying, but Oscar was one smart inventor. "Thank you." Ophelia chuckled to herself, hit the gold button, and

watched the drone take off to survey the castle. Almost instantly, Ophelia had updated plans.

She quickly examined them. It was obvious to her that the top-secret recipes would be in the location with the greatest security. And there happened to be a giant, old-fashioned iron safe (her favorite kind) just off the castle's kitchen, one room away from where she was now.

"I've got all the hiss-tory I need, Ruby! Thank you for letting me take pictures. Would you show me to the kitchen?"

During the kitchen tour, Ophelia used her superior sleight-of-paw moves and nabbed a few items. *Plastic soda bottle, hydrogen peroxide, dry yeast, dish soap, warm water, safety goggles.*

"Ophelia! I see you pilfering weird things. What are you doing?" In her ear, Oscar sounded panicked. "Just go down the hallway and get into that safe. You're only a few steps away!"

"Hallways are boring. Besides, I see a few guards hanging around. I'm about to create a teensy distraction, Oscar. Then I'll head out the window, scale the wall to the *next* window, pounce inside to nab the recipe, then scale the wall back here. Nobody will miss me."

"But why make it so complicated? Why scale when you can walk?"

"I thought you liked scales!" she chided.

Oscar didn't laugh at her attempt at a fishy joke. "No! Don't scale anything. It's unnecessary! If you really need a distraction, P.U.G. and I can easily get rid of the guards."

"No thank you," she told him firmly. "I've made up my mind. I haven't had the opportunity to use this daring heist move for quite some time. One must practice classic cat burglar moves to stay at the top of one's game." Ophelia was world-renowned for her old-fashioned ways.

She checked on her host who was in the hallway. Ruby was chatting with the security guards. Ophelia guessed she had approximately one minute to sneak out the window, scale the wall, get to the safe, and come back. If she took any longer, someone might notice that she was missing. Nobody was paying attention to her now, but she knew once they served her the dessert, all eyes would be on her, so the time was now. She sat down at a very fancy table. Under the table, she put on her safety goggles and mixed her concoction.

Suddenly, there was a chemical reaction and then . . .

Within seconds, a giant frothy geyser gushed from under the table. "Oh dear!" she exclaimed with (lovely and much dramatic) flair, to call attention to her distraction.

While everyone was running around looking for towels to clean up the mess, Ophelia ducked behind a plant, removed her disguise, and adjusted her cat burglar suit. Then, with a jeweled file and natural stealth (Stealth was, after all, her middle name), she slid open the window and hopped onto the ledge.

Once her super-suction claws were activated, she inched along the side of the castle—right into the next window.

Oscar ignored her teasing. "Hurry up!" His voice gurgled nervously. "They're going to notice you're gone! You're the guest of honor."

Ophelia wasn't worried about the few cameras she spotted since she was in her cat burglar suit and there were no guards—they were all cleaning up foam in the kitchen. It had been a little while since she'd been in an ancient castle, cracking an old-fashioned safe. She sighed with happiness.

With fifteen seconds, considerable finesse, and

a sound magnifier, she had the safe wide open. Ophelia grinned, grabbed the recipe book from its depths, and tucked it in her pocket. "Got it!" she informed Oscar.

There were only a few things to do before she made a smooth exit. She hopped back through the window and edged her way along the castle wall. In a few seconds, Ophelia was back inside the kitchen. She hid behind the plant where she'd left her Ali Kat Cooke disguise. Oscar's voice was immediately in her ear. "Okay. Now that you have the recipe book, it's time to make your great escape, Ophelia. Get out!"

She laughed. "No, no, my flustered, finned friend. I can't leave yet! I haven't tried the cake." Ophelia knew the Swiss Hiss guards would soon discover the safe had been opened, but she really did want to test the treats. But before she could change back into her Ali Kat Cooke disguise and do her tasting, a loud alarm sounded.

BRRIIINNG!

Through the leaves of the plant, she looked to

Ruby. The host's eyes were wide. "Stop! Stay right where you are!"

Time to escape. Ophelia reluctantly left her disguise behind the plant and quietly backed closer to the window. "Oscar," she whispered into her earpiece, "I don't think my helicopter is ready to go, and the front door to this castle isn't an option. I could jump out this window and run down the mountain, but ice and snow aren't my favorite. Are you still close by? Is there any chance I could get a lift down the mountain from you?"

"I don't know. . . . The velocity I'm achieving with my new skis—"

Ophelia stopped listening to the scientific jargon of her fishy inventor when the kitchen doors were flung open and security came barging in. "*Where is she?!*" they yelled. The guards scanned the room and saw Ophelia at the window.

"All right, all right!"

A big fan of good manners, Ophelia couldn't possibly leave without thanking her gracious host. Ophelia pounced over to Ruby. She pilfered a bite of cake, which melted in her mouth. "I'm so very sorry. I'm afraid I have to leave. But this tastes divine, and I'll tell the world!"

"Ophelia, hurry!" Oscar was at the window.

The guards got closer. Just before they reached her, Ophelia waved at the guards and blew a kiss to Ruby. "I'm coming through the window, sidekick."

She heard Oscar yell to P.U.G., "Catch the cat! Don't drop her! Then ski! Really fast!"

Ophelia leaped out the window. "Please don't fret, Ruby," she called as she landed in P.U.G.'s cold arms. "Your secret is safe with me! I'll return the recipe book before the weekend," she promised. "I just have one very special cake to bake!"

At Oscar's voice command, P.U.G.'s metal legs extended at the bottom to form a pair of skis. Away they went!

Ripping down the hill, the cat burglar felt just a moment of cold before her burglar suit detected the temperature change. Snow mode! Her face mask transformed into winter goggles, and she felt a blast of heat as her suit puffed up.

Behind her, Oscar provided precise instructions for the robo-dog to follow. "P.U.G.! Avoid all obstacles! Do not fall! Do not exceed seventy miles per hour. Do not allow the snowmobiles behind us to catch you." P.U.G. navigated the snowy moguls, jumps, and trees with smooth expertise.

"Our helicopter will meet us at the bottom!"
Ophelia yelled over the wind.

"They may take our action figures, but they'll never take our snazziness!"

—Ophelia von Hairball V

4

A BRAND-MEW CHALLENGE

The barking. Would. Not. Stop. P.U.G. was yipping and yapping at full volume, and Ophelia was ready to pull her fur out. She couldn't believe her fish inventor, conveniently inside his lab in the lair, was ignoring it. "Oscar!" she shouted through his door. "If you don't stop that mutt from barking, its robotic parts are going to be recycled into shiny bracelet charms that are NOT in the shape of dogs. *Or fish.*"

Oscar emerged and rolled his eyes, a bit flustered by her threat. "You don't like its voices. You don't like its barking. You really do need to be a little more tolerant of P.U.G., Ophelia. I'm trying to program it to act like a real dog!"

She was genuinely confused. "Why would you want our robot to act like a dog at all? They're so ... predictable."

Oscar looked annoyed that she would even ask. "If you must know, it's a personal challenge. Only scientists would understand. And predictable isn't always bad, Ophelia!"

With curiosity, the cat looked at the way P.U.G. was moving across the kitchen. "It just looks so fur-miliar...."

Oscar's eyes popped, and he threw back his head, laughing. "You see it! You're so observant! I've given the robo-dog a few enhanced and sophisticated dog traits modeled after the only live dog subject I have a lot of access to...." The fish bubbled and beamed.

"Oh no, you didn't," Ophelia hissed. "You're modeling its dog behavior after my nemesis and neighbor, Thug?"

"Hush your hisses. It's temporary. Please remember I'm a senior inventor, and it's my *duty* to push the boundaries of innovation." Just then, P.U.G. made a monumental drool puddle on Ophelia's priceless carpet. Oscar saw the fire in the cat's eyes. "But," Oscar added, "I'll be quickly cleaning that up and turning the dog-enhanced behavior off *right now*. In the meantime, why don't you find yourself a distraction? Bake that cake for Director MEW!"

"Oscar, you forget I'm as efficient as I am fluffy. I've already written a thank-you note to Ruby at the Swiss Hiss Confection Castle *and* baked MEW's glorious cake. In fact, the cake's been sent by special delivery to FFBI HQ." She pointed with one purr-fectly manicured paw out the window. "I deployed it the old-fashioned way—via pigeon mail!"

"Pigeon? I know you like old-fashioned, but that's terribly inefficient."

"No—it's quite efficient." She winked. "In fact, I believe the specs on that pigeon said something about 'supersonic.' I took a leap of faith that high speeds wouldn't wreck the delicate cake flavors."

Oscar narrowed his normally bulgy eyes and dashed back to his lab. Ophelia heard his safe open and close. "Ophelia! Seriously! You used my new long-distance pigeon drone invention?! It's not finished! I wanted that bird in a blue tuxedo! How did you get that out of my triple-locked lab safe?"

"Such a silly question, fish-lips. You know I've never met a safe I couldn't crack." She sat down on her ruby stool. "Please don't flip your fins about it."

PURRRR. PURRRR. Ophelia's communication station lit up. It was the FFBI call she'd been waiting for!

Her whiskers twitched with excitement. A shiny, new (big!) challenge was on the horizon.

With anticipation, Ophelia rubbed her paws together and answered the call.

On the line, Ophelia could hear some of the
FFBI agents chattering away. When her scoundrel

cousin popped on the screen, Ophelia's fur stood up with rage. She whispered to her fish inventor, "Please mute us so they can't hear us talking!" Oscar pushed the phone's mute button so she could throw her hissy fit without being heard by all the FFBI cats.

"Do you see what he's holding? My evil cousin Pierre von Rascal of Thievesylvania is *clutching* my Captain Claw-some action figure!" She raised her voice dramatically and threw her paw over her forehead in a lovely display of distress. "It greatly, greatly upsets me, fish, that he still has it. That was a gift from my grandmother. I'll never forgive Pierre for stealing it. But mark my whiskers, I'll get Captain Claw-some back."

"Something about it looks odd." Oscar isolated Captain Claw-some on-screen and enlarged the action figure so they could get a closer look. "Oh, wow!" Oscar whispered. "Ophelia, can you see that? Pierre has glued a unibrow on Captain Claw-some! Don't you think that's deranged? Your old toy's looking weird with Pierre's modifications. I'd recommend getting a whole new action figure!"

Growl. "Your suggestion that I abandon what's mine is not acceptable! Captain Claw-some belongs to me. While I can certainly understand the desire to conquer a challenge, Pierre is a rascal through and through," Ophelia answered. "He should have given it back long ago."

"He never will," Oscar said. Just then, Director MEW appeared on-screen and Oscar unmuted their phone. Ophelia's ears perked up, and she tried to forget about Captain Claw-some.

Mew continued telling the cats about the M.E.O.W. competition's rules. "You may only bring ONE item back to HQ. It must be inside the grand gallery by seven P.M. If you are early, you may choose to put your entry on display or keep it hidden from your competitors. Of course, if you think another agent has an item of greater value, you are welcome to relinquish your item, then try to replace it with something better. If you do that, you will not be allowed to have your first offering back. As a reminder, the rankings are as follows: Ophelia von Hairball V is the number one cat burglar in the world. Pierre von Rascal is ranked number two—although the FFBI advises you to watch your step, Pierre. We'll be monitoring you for unsportsmanlike behavior."

When the meeting was over, Ophelia almost sparkled with delight. "This is fabulous!"

"Fabulous? It's unfair!" Distressed, Oscar widened his bulgy eyes. "I still can't believe Pierre hasn't been kicked out of the FFBI—especially after his latest shenanigans." During a recent mission, Pierre and his bug-hating inventor, Norman, tried to sabotage Ophelia's effort to get a dangerous device. "And the nerve of Norman! It's outrageous that he still has inventor status."

Ophelia narrowed her eyes. "Pierre convinced Director MEW that he and Norman had a temporary lapse in judgment," she confided. "I don't know about Norman's past, but my cousin was a rotten scoundrel right from the start." A rare bit of remorse sparked inside her. "Maybe I

should feel a teensy bit sorry for firing Norman so quickly."

"Don't you dare feel bad!" Oscar countered. "Norman's smart enough. But he's not nice. He cheated his way through Inventor Academy. He never plays fair!"

"Sounds fur-miliar," Ophelia said, "like my cousin. They're a good match. But enough of that. It's study time." She moved to a patch of sunshine to study her latest art and jewel auction magazines.

Wearing his Small Portable Inter-Water Tank. Oscar paced. "Ophelia, I know you're the boss—but do we really have time to be lolly-gilling around? If it were up to me, we'd already be halfway through hatching a big, bold plan to steal the most valuable thing in the WORLD!"

"You know I like to have a solid research phase before I jump into any heist," Ophelia reminded him. "Can you please stop pacing? Thug and the whole Central Canine Intelligence Agency will only have to look through the front window to see that something's up." Recently, Oscar and Ophelia had discovered that Thug, a dog with the CCIA, was living *right next door*—spying on them! "We don't need them to know what we're up to."

Oscar's bulgy eyes got 20 percent bulgier, and he grinned. "Oh, don't worry, cat."

"One life is not enough to show the world
how strong, fabulous, and talented
felines are. That's why we have nine."

—Ophelia von Hairball V

5

MEWDINI (WITH FINS)

Ophelia looked at Oscar, puzzled. The inventor waved his fins triumphantly. "That's right, Ophelia. Do you want to know what that Thug mutt and the rest of the pesky CCIA will see if they look inside our window?"

Slightly curious (but mostly annoyed at Oscar's fin-terruption), Ophelia nodded. She knew she needed to practice being a better team player, so she tried to shake off her irritation. "Do tell, my fine fin-ventor."

Oscar, surprised at her interest, decided to seize the moment. "Okay! One moment, please!" He zipped into his lab. "Shut your eyes while I get into costume...."

TA-DA!

Ophelia rolled her eyes into a closed position. Recently, Oscar had been experimenting with a range of looks for himself, and Ophelia never knew what he'd dress up as next. "You look like a cheesy game show host," Ophelia told him, her good-team-player efforts already forgotten. His face fell, and she tried to fix her mistake. "But I like cheese—"

"I look like a very classy magician!" he insisted. "But never mind my outfit. Check this out."

Oscar's tablet showed the front of Ophelia's

lair—like a surveillance camera was on the house. But when the curious feline peered closer, what she saw didn't match what was *actually* happening inside: Oscar's screen showed Ophelia sleeping.

Oscar explained, "What you're seeing is real time! This is what the outside world—aka Thug and the sneaky, spying CCIA—is seeing right now."

The cat raised her eyebrows in surprise.

"That's right, Ophelia. I'm no blob fish! During my spare time, I've been diligently studying how-to videos of Mewdini—the same magician you trained with years ago. As you know, my less-than-stealthy natural fish tendencies, plus my contraptions, often prevent me from being a smooth trickster. But I'm learning all about illusions. And they can be especially powerful when combined with technology."

"Do tell," Ophelia said.

Oscar fanned his cape. "I recorded twenty-four hours of us. It's mostly just you catnapping. And I've projected that image onto the front window. If anyone looks in, they'll think they're watching us live." He tapped the screen. *"But really, they're just seeing a video.* Thug will never know we're planning an exciting international heist!"

"Brilliant!" Ophelia took Oscar's tablet for a closer look. Like Oscar said, the only thing she could see on the screen was herself in a lovely slumber. Occasionally she (elegantly) adjusted her sleep mask or (delicately) flipped her (extra-fluffy) tail. "Thug is going to give up on me." She giggled. "According to this video, I'm the most boring cat burglar in the world. Oh! Wait a second." She caught a glimpse of something else in the video and peered closer. "What's that in the background?"

Oscar's bulgy eyes blinked, and he reached for his tablet. "Oh, that? Er—uh. Nothing to see there! It's simply extra footage, for visual interest."

Ophelia clutched the tablet tighter. "Oscar, is that you lifting weights?"

"Er—maybe."

Ophelia hit the fast-forward button. In the

recording, *she* stayed sleeping, but behind her, Oscar was extra busy.

"Oh, my! And is that you solving the world's most complex math equations?"

"Er—um ... perhaps."

Ophelia hit the fast-forward button again. "And even though I hate water and have never surfed in my life, is that both of us surfing on a pool that has a wave-making machine—in my living room?" She didn't know whether to be amused or annoyed.

"Heh-heh. Um, that's what it looks like!" Oscar blushed and then he threw his fins up and grinned. "Just let me live a little, Ophelia! Isn't that your motto? Besides, just look at the beautiful teamwork happening there!" he said, longingly looking at his fake footage. "It's you and me in our matching wet suits—we're the dream team. And heaven knows your FFBI teamwork score could use a little boost! You've still got the lowest score of all the elite burglars!"

Ophelia suppressed a hiss. She hated having the lowest score *at anything*. "Regarding the fake surfing footage, I hate to burst your big bubble, but that dream is never going to happen. You *know* how I hate water."

Oscar sighed and nodded. "It's okay." He waved his fin over the tablet. "This is imagination and magic." Oscar turned his attention and his bulgy eyes away from the screen and toward Ophelia's magazine.

When MEW announced that it was mandatory she take her fin-ventor on the challenge, Oscar had churned up a record-breaking display of enthusiasm bubbles.

"Oh, fish. You're annoying me with all this 'we' talk!" She looked at his face to see his reaction. "I'm only letting you tag along to dust things. And make my snacks."

Oscar didn't disappoint. "Are you teasing me? Tell me you're teasing! I'm a senior inventor!"

"Yes. Just jokes, fish-face." She chuckled and flipped through her magazine.

"Like it or not, I'm all in on this next heist. All in! You might not know it, but you need me for this competition. So what's the most valuable thing on the planet right now?" he inquired.

"Your question, my dear seaweed breath, is the wrong one. The correct query is: What is the most valuable thing I—er, *we*—can successfully steal in the limited time we have?"

Oscar pointed to a very large photo in Ophelia's *World's Most Expensive Treasures* magazine. "Wow! *That* painting looks pretty sweet."

"Yes. *Cats Playing Cards*, by Catius Clawridge, is glorious—but it's valued so highly because it hasn't actually been seen for so long! There are rumors it was destroyed."

"Do you think Pierre and Norman are going to try to find it? Do they know something we don't know?"

"No," Ophelia told him. "There are a lot of juicy myths and legends around that painting, but it's off the table. Trust me. Pierre and Norman will try to steal a sure thing. They want to win this competition badly. I'm sure they'll just be following us to see what we're after." She closed the magazine. "In any case, we've got seventy-two hours to beat my ne-fur-ious cousin Pierre once again and to prove that I'm still at the top of my cat burglar game."

"Not just you," Oscar corrected her. "There are seventy-two hours to prove that we're the top *team*." He twirled in his cape. "Do you know the item you want us to steal?"

"Purple is the color of extravagance, creativity, royalty, luxury, peace, mystery, magic, and grandeur. Don't just wear it. Live it."

—Ophelia von Hairball V

6

CHASING SHINY OBJECTS

When Ophelia's call with international FFBI wally Simon ended, she smiled and stretched her paws above her head. "Fish-face, have you heard of the Amewthyst Scepter?"

"No."

"It was found just two weeks ago as part of a shipwreck off the coast of Italy. Rumor has it that it's a very, very valuable piece from a long-lost royal collection." Ophelia twitched her whiskers and flicked her tail dramatically. "The CCIA has some kind of interest in the treasure on that sunken ship. In fact, they've funded an expensive diving expedition. As we speak, they are pulling that treasure from the dregs of the sea. The value of the Amewthyst Scepter is extraordinary, mostly because it's very old and has a lot of *interesting* stories attached to it. If I can get my paws on it, I'll make the dogs howl. Oh, and I'll also win the M.E.O.W. competition!"

"*We! We'll* win. Teamwork, remember?"

"Right! I'm really trying my best, Oscar," she assured him.

Oscar clapped his fins together. "So are *we* going to Italy to get it?"

"Yes! My source says there's a large canine crew pulling it from the Tyrrhenian Sea today. Simon says once it's onshore, the dogs plan to hold it in a rather flimsy storage locker for approximately thirty-six hours before it's transported back to the CCIA HQ. Go ahead and pack, Oscar. I'll arrange our air transportation."

"Will we need any extraordinary gadgets or gear?" Oscar asked enthusiastically.

"I'll have my special-ops handbag," she told him. "That's got all the classic heist hardware inside. Just pack us a few good disguises!"

Within minutes, Oscar was ready. The inventor stood proudly at the door, suitcase in fin. "P.U.G.!" he ordered the robo-pooch. "I want this moment documented. I am about to officially embark on a heist with my partner, an award-winning cat burglar!"

Since P.U.G. was the most literal robot on the planet, it dropped the camera, produced a can of spray lacquer (guaranteed maximum shine), and got ready to spray the fish. "P.U.G.! STOP!" Oscar covered his S.P.I.T. and quickly edited his statement. "No! *Don't actually make me shine!* I want you to take good pictures of me!"

"I'm a big fan of shiny," Ophelia said, "but that seems extreme."

"A misunderstanding." The fish stood tall, and his eyes misted over. "This is an important photo shoot, paw-rtner. I don't know if you realize this, but it's a *very* big moment for me. It's the first time you've ever actually invited me on a heist! This time, I won't have to trick you and stow away in your travel box! I won't have to disguise myself as your pilot! This is truly a fin-tastic day."

Of course, they both knew there was only one cat who would organize such an obstacle to slow them down: a cat with an unruly unibrow called *Pierre von Rascal.*

"Fortune favors the fluffy."
—Ophelia von Hairball V

7

O.M.G.!

Oscar and Ophelia watched the dogs through the one-way glass that was her living-room window.

On her sidewalk, in the sky, and even (gasp! hiss!) lifting legs to her fancy fence, the CCIA dogs were everywhere. "If I had to make a wild guess," she growled, "I would bet my evil cousin Pierre tipped the mutts off that we are about to embark on a heist! We both know Pierre would do anything in his power to slow me down."

"They're making quite a big production out there," Ophelia told Oscar. "But their barks are worse than their bites. They can't actually do anything to prevent us from leaving." She paced back and forth. "But if they see us make an exit, they'll follow. We can't have that."

Half angry, half sad, Oscar wilted to the floor in a fishy heap. He was getting very good at dramatic poses. "Ugh! I knew we should have moved to a tropical location. Those dogs are sniffing around, and they look pretty happy. How *will* we leave undetected?"

Ophelia held out a paw to her flustered inventor. "Don't get your fins in a fret, Oscar. Have some fish-faith that a genius plan is at the tips of our claws—well, *my* claws."

Ophelia smiled slyly. "How are you doing with my new car design, Oscar?" Ophelia knew her aquatic inventor, a master of great gadgets, gear, and garb, had been working hard on creating a custom vehicle.

GENIUS PLAN?

TELL ME EVERYTHING!

"Oh, it's dandy! I was going to do a big reveal for you later this week. But if you're thinking of taking it out for a drive, I don't think it's the best idea, because Thug and the rest of the CCIA will see us when we leave, and it'll be really easy to follow us."

DISGUISES

SHOES

SPARKLES
& TREASURES

Ophelia nodded. "Yes, but if they *don't* see us leave, they can't follow us."

Oscar's wide eyes showed his exasperation. "Right . . . but they *will* see us leave!" he insisted. "At your request, your new car is 'extremely snazzy and fabulously memorable.'"

Ophelia grinned. "Would you show me this fabulous, memorable snazz-mobile?"

"It's more of a dynamic-duo-mobile," he corrected her as he led the way to the garage. "Lots of room for you *and me*. P.U.G.

GARAGE

has a good spot, too! I can show you the car now, but don't you want to wait for the big reveal party I planned? I bought seaweed snacks and teensy umbrellas for the algae punch!"

"Enough tomfishery, inventor! Show me my car!"

"One moment . . ." Oscar put on a chauffeur's hat and driving glasses. "Ta-da!" With pride, he ripped a lilac-hued cloth off the vehicle.

Instantly enthralled by her car, Ophelia gasped. "Oscar!" She gazed lovingly at her new transportation. "You've *out-inventored* yourself."

"It's true!" he proclaimed. He zipped in front of the car and opened the hood. "Let me show you what she does."

Ophelia jumped into the car and patted the passenger spot. "Don't stand in front of it, fish. Close the hood and hop in beside me."

"Uh, okay—" Oscar climbed in. "You need to name this car. And naturally, there are a lot of gadgets to learn." Ophelia saw several gold buttons. These were Oscar's specialty—he put outrageous (sometimes slightly dangerous) "bonus" functions in all his designs. "Let me show you how everything works."

Ophelia's brain was moving a mile a minute. "I've got it! She'll be called *the Ophelia Mew-bile Go!* And while I'd love to hear how the O.M.G. works, we just don't have time right now."

"Why don't we have time?" Oscar asked.

"We now have exactly seventy-two hours to pilfer our treasure and get it to FFBI HQ in Brussels. We've really got to go!" She patted the steering wheel with a paw. "I'm so excited to drive this."

Oscar looked confused. "But the O.M.G. isn't

completely ready. I haven't worked the bugs out of some of the very special gold features yet." Stubborn, he crossed his fins over his chest. "In any case, like I said, we can't simply *drive* out of here, cat! Thug and the CCIA will see us as soon as we exit the garage! They'll follow us to the airport."

WE'RE **NOT** LEAVING FROM THE GARAGE, SILLY.

HUH? HOW ARE WE LEAVING?

Her eyes sparkled mischievously. "Over the last little while, I've secretly been making some very interesting additions to the lair." Ophelia turned the key in the ignition and started the O.M.G. "Oh. She purrs!"

"Of course she purrs! Ophelia, exactly what have you built into this lair?"

"I'm going to show you." From her special-ops handbag, Ophelia pulled out a remote control, then pushed a button. The wall in front of them opened to reveal a long, dark tunnel. Oscar gasped.

"Are you ready to go now?" Ophelia put on her sunglasses. "I'm traveling light. I *cannot wait* to drive this car up the Italian coastline!"

"Wait!" a flustered Oscar yelled. "I need my suitcase! I've got a few new styles that are perfect for the Italian fashion scene. Oh, and we need P.U.G.!"

Ophelia gave Oscar time to grab his case, and P.U.G. hopped in.

"I don't feel fully prepared, Ophelia," Oscar fretted. "I imagined having more time to pack for my first sanctioned heist. Also"—he peered up ahead—"where does this tunnel come out?"

"Several miles from the house. It will get us directly to the top floor of a private airport parkade. The CCIA has no idea it's here."

"Wow." Oscar whistled, surprised at how fast this all was moving. "So once we're out of the lair undetected—then what?"

"Then we drive ourselves up a big ramp onto a luxury plane bound for Italy. When we get there, we'll cruise up the coast, slip past the CCIA dogs, get the Amewthyst Scepter from the storage locker, and head to the FFBI in Brussels, Belgium. There will still be time for hat shopping before we claim our prestigious M.E.O.W. competition trophy. It's a purr-fect plan, and we're going to win. As we always do."

"Life is full of twists and turns.
I like to take them at full speed,
with confidence, and without dogs."

—Ophelia von Hairball V

8

TUNNEL VISION

With Oscar in the passenger seat and P.U.G. in the back, Ophelia drove through the winding underground tunnel.

"When did you arrange to have this built?" Oscar's voice was bursting with emotion. "Don't get me wrong. I'm really excited we're on our way. But I can't believe you kept *this* project a secret from me." He pouted. "It's kind of a big deal."

She turned toward him and winked. "You don't always know what I've got up my fashionable sleeve, fish. I started thinking about building a secret tunnel as soon as we discovered that Thug, our not-so-good neighbor, was with the CCIA."

"You could have asked me to manage this project," Oscar scolded her. "I would have had P.U.G. do all the digging—it's proven itself a great digger!"

"You were too busy creating this amazing O.M.G.," Ophelia said as she glanced at P.U.G. It was acting like a real dog, sticking its head out the window and panting. "But you're right. Next time, we'll ask the metal mutt. Wouldn't it be funny if we told it to start digging—and then we forgot to tell it to stop? I guess its batteries would eventually run out—"

"Ugh! P.U.G. has no batteries, Ophelia. I keep telling you that! Just admit you'd miss the robotic masterpiece if it were gone!"

"Hmmm." She grinned.

Oscar rolled his bulgy eyes at Ophelia. "Do you think we totally dodged Thug?"

"I suspect, for now, Thug is in the dark, but there will be more dogs in Italy. In any case, the more we can do to slow them down, the better off we are. I must say, it's quite a challenge to keep ahead of both Pierre *and* those mutts. Being a mastermind cat burglar with competition isn't easy."

A dark shadow enveloped them as the car approached a wall. Ophelia slowed the O.M.G. down and then hit the remote. The wall opened for her to drive through. The trio emerged from the tunnel onto the third floor of a parking garage!

"I had one of my allies do some work in this airport garage as it was being built," Ophelia explained. "It wasn't hard to make a secret little room here and link it to my tunnel."

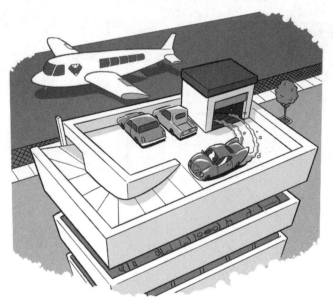

Oscar nodded, impressed. Once outside, they drove down the parking ramp and directly into the cargo area of the FFBI plane that was waiting for them. Soon they were settled in, headed to Italy.

On the way, Ophelia took the opportunity to give Oscar some basic burglary training. She made sure P.U.G. recorded all the best teamwork moments so she could send them to MEW.

"When we land," Ophelia told him, "assume we are being followed. Of course, we will take precautions."

"Followed by whom?" Oscar sounded scared. "Pierre and Norman should be busy doing their own heist. And the CCIA shouldn't know we're here."

"Do you remember how Pierre tricked us in Paris? And fish-napped you?" Oscar gulped and nodded. "Do you remember Egypt? Vancouver? New York? When he almost got that terrible catastrophic device?" Oscar nodded harder. "Pierre is evil and sloppy, but he's also resourceful. And more than anything, he wants to win my top cat burglar title. I would be very surprised if he wasn't following us. And the dogs—they're soooo loyal to their ideas! They'd like nothing more than to capture me and shut the FFBI down. Can you even imagine, Oscar, a world in which there were no cat burglars? No wonderful time-honored traditions? No chance to prove our sassy stealth?"

Oscar shook his head. Now that he was finally

an official sidekick, he didn't want the magic to end. "We will prevail! Just tell me what to do."

"Follow my lead. We're going to liberate the Amewthyst Scepter from a storage locker near the sea. It'll be exactly like an old-fashioned safe—but it may have several guard dogs on duty." Oscar straightened his collar, and Ophelia sensed his concern. "No fear, fish. We could handle those pesky guard dogs in our sleep."

PURRRR. PURRRR. Her ringtone was unmistakable. "Yes?" Ophelia answered on speaker. It was Simon.

"The name is Hairball.
Ophelia von Hairball V."

—Ophelia von Hairball V

9
FISH À LA MODE

*T*he bottom of the sea? *Worst place ever!* Ophelia released a hiss. She thanked Simon for the information, then took a moment to think. She knew
she didn't *need* the Amewthyst Scepter. After all,
around the globe were many amazing and very
valuable trinkets and treasures she could nab and
use to win the M.E.O.W. competition and keep
her title as the number one cat burglar. But the

truth was, as soon as she'd heard about the scepter, she'd wanted it *very badly*. It was purple! It was sparkly! And it had cute ears! Also, the fact that the CCIA wanted it made it that much more tantalizing. But, desirable or not, the jeweled scepter was deep down in the water—and there was *nothing* she hated more than water.

Ophelia looked over at Oscar, who was already hard at work with a notebook and some big dreams, schemes, and disguises. One of his sketches sparked an idea that caused her whiskers to twitch. "Oscar, please tell me about the biggest and best features of the O.M.G."

Oscar rubbed the top of his S.P.I.T., ready to impress the unimpressible feline. "Your vehicle has all the usual features and modes you'd want."

"Do tell!"

"All right." He straightened his tie and took a big gulp of water. "This is simply a selection of the modes we have available: accordion mode, alien mode, bathroom-stall mode, bubblegum mode, caterpillar-glam mode, cloak mode, cuppa-tea mode, flamethrower mode, freeze mode, garden gnome mode, junk mode, kiwi mode, leprechaun mode, mime mode, outfit-match mode, pyramid mode, rocket mode, silent mode, sneeze mode, toxic mode, yeti mode, yoga mode, ta-da mode . . ."

Since it seemed like the fish was going to go on for eternity (and Ophelia didn't *actually* have nine lives to wait for him to finish), she interrupted. "Pardon me, Oscar, but did you perchance build a deep-sea-diving submarine mode into the car?"

She held her breath. The (brave) cat burglar in

her hoped he'd say yes. But the (tiny) scaredy-cat part of her hoped he'd say no.

Oscar grinned, then reached inside the glove box and pushed a gold button. "Introducing one of my favorite modes—*pirate* mode! With one push of *this* gold button, your car transforms into a legendary aquatic adventure machine equipped for pilfering treasure from under the sea!" He pointed a fin at himself. "Just like this guy." Oscar gave himself a moment to shine and then added, "But it's not *quite* feature complete."

Ophelia nodded and tried to ignore the bubbling fear inside her. *I want to beat Pierre more than I want to stay away from the water.* Her fur floofed with forced bravado. "Well done, Oscar. Let's test that aquatic mode out, shall we? I anticipate that with a bit of clever planning, we will soon have the very lovely Amewthyst Scepter in our claws—"

"And our fins!" Oscar added enthusiastically.

"And our paws!" P.U.G. piped up robotically.

When the plane touched down in Italy, Ophelia, Oscar, and P.U.G. drove off its ramp. In convertible mode, Ophelia wove expertly through traffic along the Italian coastline. The sea sparkled. Everything seemed to be going smoothly . . . *too smoothly?*

She kept looking in her rearview mirror but didn't see anything suspicious. *Where is Pierre right*

now? She fully expected him to be following her so he could steal her prize and win her title. "P.U.G.," she ordered the robot in the backseat, "please keep your eyes out for Pierre."

The robot unscrewed its eyes and flung them out of the car. They rolled off the cliff and into the sea.

"Ophelia! Please watch what you tell it to do. P.U.G. is very literal," Oscar reminded her. "Thankfully, P.U.G. has extra parts." The inventor pushed a button, and another set of eyes popped out of P.U.G.'s complex circuitry.

With speed and expertise, Ophelia maneuvered closer to their dock destination. Her old-fashioned moves seemed to work nicely with Oscar's newfangled car technology.

In the passenger seat, feeling like a full-fledged sidekick, Oscar was terribly excited. "I really cannot wait to win this prize with you. So far, this is a purr-fect heist! We got to use your new car! There are modes for evey occasion! And with its pirate mode—a car-submarine hybrid—I'm about to help save the day. This is all going smoothly. And as much as you—"

"I'm sorry, fish, to interrupt. But I must share that I'm getting suspicious. We haven't even seen a glimpse of Pierre."

"You're right!" Oscar grew thoughtful. "So far, no Pierre and no Norman. Maybe we're just lucky?"

Hmmm. If Pierre hadn't followed them, it meant he had *his own* plans. But Pierre never had his own plans, because he was always stealing hers! Ophelia felt unsettled, and her fur prickled. "Fish, first things first. Please take a selfie of the three of us and send it to Director MEW. I want her to see this outstanding, happy teamwork thing we're doing!"

"Done!" Oscar told her.

"Excellent." Ophelia grinned. Teamwork wasn't as hard as it sounded. And she was getting a LOT of nice photos out of the deal. "Now, take my mind off Pierre by explaining the waterproof submarine capabilities of my car."

OF COURSE.

WE'VE GOT A **STATE-OF-THE-ART SUBMARINE SYSTEM** HERE. OR, AS I LIKE TO CALL IT: S.A.S.S.

"In any case, I'm afraid air isn't our top worry right now," Oscar continued, "because when I was doing surveillance to find the exact location of the shipwreck, I saw something else: About one mile in front of us, there are dogs *everywhere*. I assume it's CCIA security. And"—he blinked furiously—"I think I even saw Thug!"

Ophelia's eyes narrowed. She was getting rather tired of her nosy neighbor trying to ruin her fun! It was high time to wreck some of his.

"Shiny things are nice, but it's much better to have inner shine. That goes with every handbag."

—Ophelia von Hairball V

10

DOGGONE IT, ANYHOW

A winding road that ran almost parallel to the dock allowed them to get close to the dive site without being spotted. As they approached their target destination, there was loud, hyper barking, sounds of fire-hydrant delight, and the distinct smell of half-chewed, slobbery liver biscuits. Ophelia rolled her eyes. *Dogs are just so yucky.*

Oscar's intel had been spot-on—by the dock, mutts were absolutely *everywhere*.

Ophelia watched with curiosity as Thug expertly commanded a pack of dogs to patrol the area. "They're trying to make sure nobody gets near enough to see what they're doing. For some reason, they *really* want this treasure. Too bad he's a canine," Ophelia lamented, "because that dog Thug is *good*."

On the dashboard, Oscar flipped a switch. "Stealth mode has been activated. Without it, the dogs will sniff us out. How on earth—or on the high seas—are we going to get around these mutts?"

Deep in thought, Ophelia flicked her tail. "Let's

not get around them." Oscar tilted his little head, puzzled. "*Occam's razor*, my dear fish."

"Huh?"

"Occam's razor is sometimes called 'the rule of simplicity.' It means the best solution to a problem is probably the simplest one."

Oscar nodded. "So, in this particular case, our problem is a pack of pesky dogs. Instead of us finding a complicated way around them . . ." He trailed off, deep in thought. It didn't take him long to figure it out. "Let's just find a way to make them go away!" He laughed. "I like this 'simple' rule. But, Ophelia"—he looked concerned—"they seem really focused on their duty of guarding the dock."

"I know I told you to turn down P.U.G.'s Thugness before. But can you turn it up again, please?"

"You mean make P.U.G. act *more* like a dog?"

"You know it kills me to say that," Ophelia growled. "But yes. And, more precisely, more like *Thug*. So slobbery! So tediously rule-abiding! And put a hat on its head. We need every CCIA dog to think P.U.G. is Thug. The robot will lead them away, and we can get onto the dock and closer to our treasure."

"Let's do it!" The fin-ventor accessed P.U.G.'s program and dug in his fish-case to pull out an extra hat. "Ta-da!"

Ophelia assessed P.U.G. "Looks like Thug's twin. Just so you know, in any other circumstance, two Thugs would be enough to make me climb the curtains."

Oscar laughed. "I know. It won't happen again. As an added bonus, I already have Thug's voice stored. P.U.G. will *sound* like Thug, too!"

"Excellent. Now wait for the real Thug to go to his command center. Then we'll release P.U.G. and give these dogs a *new kind* of paw and order.

Please instruct P.U.G. to get the dogs away from here. Maybe they can do the weird, silly chasing thingy dogs like to do." She rolled her eyes. "When P.U.G. and the others are AWOL, we'll submerge the O.M.G., turn it into the S.A.S.S., nab the Amewthyst Scepter ASAP, then be on our way to FFBI HQ to win the M.E.O.W. competition!"

With a few excited barks, P.U.G. (disguised as Thug) was able to distract the dogs from their posts. As they all pounced and panted away, the trio removed their disguises and got into the O.M.G. Ophelia drove right up the dock until they were perched at the edge of the sea.

CAT, YOU SURE USE A LOT OF ACRONYMS.

"Are you sure this is going to work?" Ophelia's heart pounded.

"Of course it'll work! I'm the best gilled gadget guru on the planet." He gestured toward their reflection in the water. "Look at us! The dynamic duo. The dream team!" With a smile, he reached across

Ophelia, hit the gold button on the dashboard, and the O.M.G. transformed into the S.A.S.S.—the state-of-the-art submarine system Oscar had promised.

With hardly a splash, they entered the water and were quickly submerged. On the back of the vehicle, the propellers started to hum. On the front, a bright beam lit up the darkness. "My calculations tell me that the ship is stuck on a ridge a little ways from the dock. This aquatic version of your car goes about as fast as any first-class submarine, so we'll reach the bottom quickly," Oscar said.

"If you're ever asked to go out on a limb, make sure your claws are sharp, your fur is fluffed, and there aren't rosebushes (or water) beneath you."

—Ophelia von Hairball V

11

PURR-FECT PIRATES

All the shiny sunken treasure almost made Ophelia forget her watery fears. "Look at it sparkle! It's so glorious! And there's the Amewthyst Scepter!" she exclaimed. She'd read about it and seen pictures. It was bigger than she thought it would be, a magnificent glowing purple scepter. "Okay, fish. It's your time to shine. Get out there and grab it!" she told him.

Oscar looked at her, confused. "Um . . . grab it?"

"Yes! I presume you've got some sort of underwater pod or, better yet, a slick, sleek, electronic claw-y thing on the bottom of this S.A.S.S. for the purpose of grabbing treasure?"

Oscar grimaced. "Well, that's the thing I was trying to tell you before. That's what I meant by 'not quite feature complete.' I didn't get as far as adding a claw to this design model. And there's no airtight escape hatch."

"Well! The good news is that we can definitely get the treasure!" Oscar tried to force some optimism into his voice.

"And the bad news?" Ophelia prompted him.

"The bad news is that we're one hundred percent going to get into the water, and we *will* have to swim in the weeds."

A sharp hiss escaped her mouth. "Do you have my waterproof suit?"

"I do, of course. In fact, we have matching suits."

Ophelia paused for a moment. She stared at the purple Amewthyst Scepter right below them. She didn't want to go in the water!

"Our air is getting low. If we're going to dive for the scepter, we've got to do it now." The cat was frozen. "Ophelia! How badly do you want it?"

Ophelia snorted. "You know the answer to that." Her heart was pounding so hard, she thought Oscar could probably see it.

The cat burglar closed her eyes and gulped. Outside the S.A.S.S., the water would surround her. It was dark and murky. Just the thought of it made her feel claw-strophobic.

"You really can do this, Ophelia," he told her again quietly. "And I'm not just saying that because I want to be your sidekick. Or because I want to win this heist. I've seen you do really, really hard things. This isn't hard. It's just something you're not used to. But I can help! That's what paw-rtners are for." Oscar looked nervously at the clock and waited for her decision.

Ophelia nodded. "Let's do it, fish." She suited up. Before she could change her mind, Oscar clipped her belt to the S.A.S.S. and opened the hatch. Water flooded in, and Ophelia froze.

Oscar nodded to her and gave her a fins-up. Then he grabbed her paw and glided through the water at a super speed toward the purple gem. Ophelia couldn't believe she was in the depths of the sea. She was touching seaweed—*and still alive*. She felt her panic subside and instinctively moved her paw to grab the glorious treasure but then stopped herself. She gestured to her fish inventor. Oscar should be the one to take it. After all, his magnificent creations and (bizarre) love of water were the reasons she was even this close to victory.

Ophelia nodded. More than anything, she wanted to feel dry and fluffy. "What exactly did you instruct the robot to do?"

"I told it to take those mutts around the block a couple times!"

"A couple times? Did you actually say 'a couple'? As in two?"

Oscar grimaced. "Eeek. Yes. I guess I should

have told it a really big number." They both knew that P.U.G. would have followed those instructions *exactly*. "I guess we better be prepared because the CCIA dogs will be waiting for us when we emerge. I'd prefer that we find a different dock, but we don't have enough air to look for one. I'd be fine, but you'd be a goner!"

"Dogs or no dogs, just get us to dry land," Ophelia told him. "I'll figure out the rest."

Oscar maneuvered them back to the S.A.S.S. and they shot up to the surface to meet the dogs—and their fate.

"Some say to let sleeping dogs lie.
Fine, but while you're doing that,
tie all their shoelaces together."

—Ophelia von Hairball V

12

FIN-DERS KEEPERS

The S.A.S.S. surfaced at the dock just before its air ran out. There was a heavy CCIA presence, but Ophelia let out a sigh of relief as she stepped out of the car and back on solid ground.

"Happy to be back on terra firma?" Oscar inquired.

"Terra fur-ma is where it's at," Ophelia replied slyly. Under the bright dock lights, the Amewthyst

Scepter was spectacular. As predicted, P.U.G. was back on the dock, looking blissfully clueless. Thug sat right beside his robotic twin. Both panted. Behind them, a sea of CCIA dogs blocked any chance of an easy escape.

"Well, well." When Ophelia and Oscar emerged from their S.A.S.S., a smug-looking Thug stepped forward. Ophelia did enjoy his confidence—and his old-fashioned fedora.

Ophelia fluffed and shook the remaining water droplets off her fur.

The dog continued. "I was going to say we've got to stop meeting like this, but it's getting rather fun. We've caught you red-pawed, Ophelia von Hairball V. There are over one hundred CCIA dogs here who are witnesses to your crime. That Amewthyst Scepter is not yours, and we shall finally, FINALLY stop you in your overly confident tracks." He glanced at Oscar. "You and your little finned accomplice, that is. I will make an example of you both."

Oscar started to shake. "Ophelia!" he moaned softly. "I didn't think this whole sidekick thing through. I only considered the fun parts of the heists. But I didn't think about getting caught."

The dogs began to murmur. Thug opened his mouth. For a moment, nothing came out (except a bit of drool). After a moment, he tried again. "But— but we were here first!"

"Where?" Ophelia chuckled. "On the dock? Silly dog, the shipwreck is outside the boundary of any country, so it's not your property. Since my esteemed fish and I got the scepter first—of our own volition—we've decided to claim it." Ophelia's eyes narrowed. "Of course, you are welcome to dispute this. You may or may not win. But let's be honest. It would be a waste of time. Because by the time you do the paperwork and the courts decide the rightful owners, I'll have returned the loot anyway." She winked. "As I always do."

Thug shook, and his ears went flat to his head.

"Try not to be too angry," the feline continued. "There are a lot of other beautiful things down there for you to claim. But for now, my colleagues and I need to be going. We've got a rather important appointment."

Thug and the CCIA dogs couldn't do a thing while Ophelia, Oscar, and P.U.G. drove away with the sparkling scepter. The trio's destination was FFBI HQ in Brussels.

They thought they were home free.

"Whoever said 'it's better to be safe than sorry' was probably a canine who never bothered with impossible heists, helicopter escapes, or double-dog dares."

—Ophelia von Hairball V

13

HISS-TORIC MEW-MENTS

F FBI HQ was a tall, sleek building of glass and steel with plenty of sunny napping spots, deluxe scratching posts, dispensers that gave out free catnip, and a paw meow-ssage therapist who came in twice a week.

Ophelia and Oscar left P.U.G. on the main floor with all the other robotic helpers and then headed up an elevator to the gallery. The gallery was where all the elite cat burglar agents had their treasures on display in hopes of winning the M.E.O.W. competition. Ophelia was curious to see the treasures other elite agents had stolen.

"This was the best heist of my life," Oscar said with dreamy enthusiasm. Side by side, they walked through the building's tight security.

"Wasn't it the *only* heist of your life?"

"Well, I've been on a few now—but I guess this is my first legitimate one." He grinned. "And it's been everything I've ever hoped for and more! I was involved every step of the way! I designed the car, the disguises ..." He pulled out the photo collection. "Plus, I even have photo evidence of our fabulous teamwork moments." He looked to Ophelia, his adoration gushing from every scale. "And now, best paw-rtner ever, we're going to win top prize! That's right—*you and me*! We've even got a few hours left! We're the ultimate pair."

With the Amewthyst Scepter wrapped in one of Oscar's purple velvet scarves, they walked down a maze of hallways. Through a set of glass doors, Ophelia caught a glimpse of Pierre and Norman. They were looking far too comfortable and confident for Ophelia's liking. Once again, she couldn't squash a nagging feeling that there was something *not quite right*. Pierre should have been hot on her tail the whole time. Yet here he was—very early and very smug.

Ophelia and Oscar showed their security passes, which opened the doors to the inner gallery. When they entered, cats were admiring the spoils—the pedestals were almost full.

For a moment, Ophelia forgot Pierre, and her eyes swept the room to appraise the items. Her confidence swelled. Paws down, the Amewthyst Scepter beat everything in the room.

"Here's where we put our treasure!" Oscar declared.

Ophelia put the wrapped Amewthyst Scepter on the pedestal and stepped back to take a breath. They'd finished the competition early! "Wait. What's this?" Ophelia asked. "Why does our name-plate say 'O²'?"

"Oh." Oscar blushed. "I submitted our official team name." He did a halfhearted grimace. "I guess I forgot to tell you." He noted the annoyed swishing of her tail. "But to make up for it, I'll show you something quite wonderful!" Oscar reached down into his fish-case and pulled out two T-shirts.

He wriggled into his custom T-shirt, then held Ophelia's up to her. "Ta-da! Our O² team uniforms! And this is just the beginning!"

"Oscar," she hissed, "I hate to burst *all your bubbles*, but except as part of a disguise, I've never worn a T-shirt in my life!" She looked up and saw FFBI Director MEW peering down at them from an office up above. Thinking about her teamwork score, she ripped the anger off her face and forced some kind words through clenched teeth. "But thank you so much for the effort."

"You might as well put it on!" Oscar insisted with ample enthusiasm. "Then we can take a picture together and put it all over Instacat!"

Ophelia didn't move.

"Oh, please, please, please wear it," he insisted. He held up the shirt to Ophelia and started to snap photos of the two of them. "It would make me feel like you really believed in teamwork—and we both know how much you want to win that title...."

Just then, Pierre cut behind them and ruined the last picture. "Well, hellooooo, cousin Ophelia!" Pierre sneered, his unibrow caving inward. "It's *so* great to see you got out of your little dog-infested neighborhood to be part of the big competition. Hopefully they'll give out participation medals to the losers so you can go home with *something*." His laugh was sinister.

Norman joined it. Oscar took off his O² shirt and straightened his tie.

"And of course you brought your little aquatic fan-fish. It'll be so much fun to see you *both lose*."

Ophelia wasn't in the mood for their rudeness. "You're looking particularly crooked today." She sneered at Pierre, gesturing to his top hat. He straightened his hat, then his jacket. As he moved, the top of Captain Claw-some popped out of his pocket.

Ophelia wasn't pleased to see Captain Clawsome was showing signs of wear and tear. It wasn't surprising—Pierre didn't take care of anything.

Pierre pivoted on his paws and walked a few feet in front of them. He beckoned Ophelia to follow him to a pedestal marked THE AMAZING PIERRE VON RASCAL. "And Norman" had been added as an afterthought. Ophelia wanted to ignore Pierre and show him that she didn't care about his treasure, but the cat's intense curiosity got the best of her.

Ophelia walked over to the pedestal to look at what they'd entered into the competition but was disappointed. All she saw was a rectangle covered in heavy red fabric. Ophelia guessed they were concealing a painting. "What's this?" she asked.

Pierre's inventor, Norman, stepped out from behind Pierre. "None of your business, cat! And"— he blinked furiously—"since you're going to lose badly, I made little medals for you and your incompetent fish. In case you are wondering, they're *not* real gold." Pierre and Norman looked at each other and laughed.

Ophelia let the rude comment slide off her fuzzy back.

But Oscar was upset, and he didn't try to hide

it. "Wow! You're so mean, Norman. You should try being nicer once in a while. It would make you feel better about yourself."

Ophelia took a deep breath and tried to push down the hissy fit that threatened to stand all her fur on end. Norman had been Ophelia's sixteenth inventor. One of the reasons she'd rejected him was because of his annoying knock-knock jokes. She'd managed to get rid of him by exploiting his fear of bugs. After leaving her, Norman had teamed up with Pierre—and the FFBI had assigned Oscar to her.

"Don't you think your confidence level is just a bit premature?" Ophelia asked. "I'm always a fan of patting yourself on the back, but you don't even know what treasure we have to enter into the contest!" Pierre didn't even blink.

Ophelia hid her frustration and shrugged. She didn't want Pierre to know that her curiosity about what was under the red fabric was killing her.

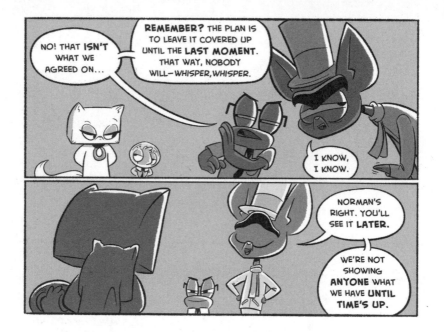

Ophelia and Oscar went to their pedestal area and took the Amewthyst Scepter out of its lilac velvet draping. She carefully watched Pierre's face as she set it up on the display. There was no surprise, no anger, and no fear on his face.

Ophelia was worried. She was starting to think that whatever Pierre and Norman had stolen, it was worth *more* than the scepter. Unless she did something quickly, Pierre was going to win the prize!

"E=MC²: where *E* is Expectations and *MC* is Much Catnip."

—Ophelia von Hairball V

14

SOMETHING FISHY

Ophelia's heart pounded, and frustration rose in her chest. "Oscar," she whispered, "I don't think Pierre is bluffing. We need to find out exactly what Pierre and Norman have under that red cloth. Then we're going back out to steal something that's worth more."

Oscar's eyes opened so big, Ophelia was afraid they might pop. "What? Why?"

"Because right now I'm pretty sure they've got us beat."

Oscar frowned and shook his fin back and forth. "Oh, no they don't! I *will not* be losing my first official heist competition," he told her with fish fury. "I'll send one of my tiny drone cameras to peek under the blanket and report back." He grinned. "And just for Norman," he said, "I'll use the bumblebee one!"

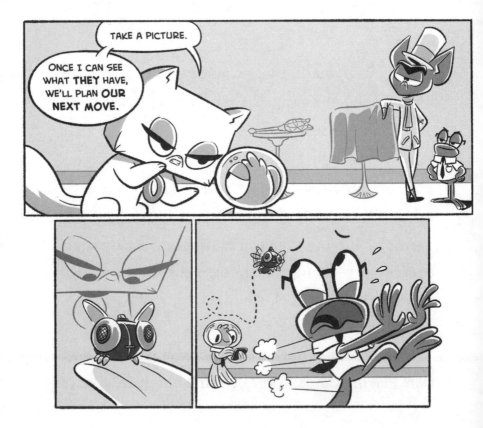

The pair made their way down to the lobby of FFBI HQ. "What is it, Ophelia?" Oscar fretted. Ophelia *never* seemed defeated!

"I'm all right, fish. I just need to pause and reflect for a moment." Ophelia sat down on a bench and gestured for Oscar to sit beside her.

"Do you remember the magazine I showed you before we went to Italy? It had the world's most valuable treasures?"

"Sure do."

"The number one most expensive painting was *Cats Playing Cards.* You asked me about it." Oscar nodded. "Well," she told him, "that's what they've got."

"How? You said that painting was only a legend!" Oscar struggled to understand.

"Well, there is no record of it in any mew-seum or private art collection."

"But, Oscar," she whispered, "I happen to know without a shadow of a doubt that the *Cats Playing Cards* painting is real and has not been destroyed! Also, it's priceless and there's not a shred of hope that we will find something worth more in the short time we have left."

Tears welled in Oscar's bulgy eyes. "So that's it? There's no way for Team O² to win?" He tried to control the shaking in his voice. "But this is my first heist, Ophelia. *I cannot fail.* You're my *team.* I'll be upset forever if I let you down!" Oscar's shaking gave way to sadness. He flopped down on the bench and stared at the ceiling. "What will I do?"

"You're very good at dusting?" Ophelia teased. But when Oscar's tears started to splash inside his S.P.I.T., she turned serious. "Fish, please! Stop the waterworks! *Of course* there's a way to win! You keep telling me you're the smartest gilled gadget and gear inventor on the planet. Don't forget you're paw-rtnered with the most skilled and celebrated cat burglar in the universe!"

"But you just said that we won't find something worth more than that painting."

"We won't." Ophelia grinned. "But Pierre's painting—the one under that red velvet drape up there in the gallery, anyway—is one hundred percent *fake*! That's not the real *Cats Playing Cards.*"

Oscar's fish lips formed a perfect O.

"And we, my fine finned paw-rtner, just need to prove it."

"I can't even believe it! How can you be so sure

the painting Pierre and Norman have is a forgery?" Oscar asked.

"Because I happen to have solid intel on where the real painting is. I may have even pounced over it a time or two...."

A puzzled Oscar thought for a moment, then sat up. "Well," he said, "then all we have to do is run upstairs and tell Director MEW about it. That's easy!"

"I'm afraid," Ophelia explained, "it's not that simple."

"Why not?"

The cat and fish made their way back into the gallery. "Because Pierre and Norman wouldn't have submitted it if they thought anyone could prove it was a fake."

"Always be the cat's meow: Don't point out a problem unless you also purr-pose a purr-fectly fabulous solution."

—Ophelia von Hairball V

15

FUR-GERY 101

O scar stared at her. "What do you mean, they've been plotting this for a long time?"

Ophelia stopped pacing in front of Oscar. "Is Norman an artist?" she asked. "Do they teach any painting classes at Inventor Academy?"

"There are lots of classes," Oscar said. "And while I can't say whether Norman is a gifted artist, he was in my Forgery 101 class, and I barely squeaked ahead of him for top marks."

"What did the class teach you?"

Oscar tried to remember. "Mostly we learned how to use science to test if a painting was a forgery."

"Please, tell me more!" Ophelia said.

"Well, if you've got an exceptional artist and a lot of patience, any painting style can be faked," Oscar told her. "But besides the art style, there are other, scientific ways to detect and prove a forgery."

"How?" Ophelia asked, now impatient.

"The best way is to test the paint and paper or canvas. Paints from certain time periods have certain chemical compounds. We also learned how to age-test paper or canvas to determine its authenticity."

"And since you also took that course, do tell me, fish . . . if you were planning a very clever forgery, what would you do?"

"Hmmm," Ophelia replied thoughtfully. "I'd

do the same. I suppose with enough practice, you'd get the technique right." She looked at her paws. "Though I'm not a fan of messing up my manicured claws."

Oscar laughed. "Despite these awkward-looking fins, I'm fairly artistic. Of course, the painting technique is only part of it. The other thing to consider is the materials. You need everything to match the original process. If it were me, I'd hunt for paper or canvas that was the same age as the painting I wanted to forge. I'd also get other paintings by that artist and test the chemical makeup of the paint so I could re-create it—probably in my lab."

"Precisely!" Ophelia said, impressed.

"I will assume Norman is clever enough to have done all of that with the *Cats Playing Cards* painting, so it will be im-paw-ssible to prove it's a forgery. Every test they do will show that it's probably the real thing." She shook her head, but then a smile slowly spread over her face. "The one they've got is framed, right?"

Oscar took a breath. "I have an idea! Maybe we should just go tell Director MEW everything. She can come with us to look at the real painting?"

Ophelia smiled. "No, no. Director MEW doesn't have time to run around Europe to look at mew-seum floors." She knew her next statement would shock her fish inventor. "But I have a lovely solution. It's as bold as I am! We're just going to have to steal *the whole mew-seum.*"

Oscar's S.P.I.T. filled with bubbles as he burst into laughter. "I can't believe what you're saying, cat! Stealing a whole mew-seum in another country is a really big deal. We don't have the time—or even a plan!"

"Perhaps we *are* lacking a few things," Ophelia admitted with a confident grin. "But what we lack in plans and time, we make up for with ingenuity and grit! Besides, it's a *small* building. And we won't be moving it on our own. . . . We're going to get lots of help!"

Oscar took a big breath. He was learning to trust the cat's instinct. "If the plan is to steal an entire—albeit small—mew-seum, we'd better hurry up and leave right now!" Oscar said.

Ophelia knew he was right. Time was short, and stakes were high. "Fish inventor: Are you ready to take a chance with me to win this competition?" she asked.

"I think so." Oscar gulped.

"All right, then. You need to understand the risk. Before we leave the building, I'm going to have to relinquish the Amewthyst Scepter and pull it from the competition." Tail flicking, she leaned over and looked him in the eyes. "The official M.E.O.W. competition rules state that if we go to get a second item, we give up the first one. That means if we don't get the mew-seum, we will have nothing."

Oscar's eyes bulged. He nodded. "I understand." His voice was strangled. "Let's do whatever it takes to beat Pierre and Norman—and win the title we deserve. O^2 is the dream team!"

"Whenever a door closes, a window opens.
And it's a lot of fun when that window leads
to an emerald ring, a priceless statue,
or a cushy spot in the sunshine."

—Ophelia von Hairball V

16

AYE, AYE, CAPTAIN!

It almost hurt Ophelia to hand over the sparkling Amewthyst Scepter to a very surprised Director MEW. "I'm officially relinquishing this. I'm—*we're*—off to get something different."

"This is quite a rare item," MEW said. "In fact, there is a rich hiss-tory with this, and there are rumors that…" She trailed off and raised an eyebrow. "I'm sure you know the rumors."

"I do. And there is no doubt that fabulous scepter deserves a fabulous set of paws to be holding it," Ophelia confirmed. "But my fish-face—I mean, my teammate and I have something else in mind. Would you keep it safe for now?"

MEW nodded. "Your time is limited."

"I'm ready for action! We've got precisely three hundred and fifty minutes!" Oscar piped up, and the pair exited the gallery.

Ophelia was silent down the stairs, and just as they reached the main floor atrium, she stopped abruptly. *Hmm ... there is one very important, extra mission to do before we leave the building.* Her idea would require Oscar's tech-savvy know-how, plus a few old-fashioned cat burglar moves.

"I could," Oscar admitted hesitantly, "but what you're really asking is if I can hack into the FFBI system." His eyes were wide. "And since it could cost me my FFBI status and I could go to *prison*, there would have to be a very good reason to try such a thing! Besides, it will require a lot of speedy skill. There are extreme countermeasures in place. I should know," he added. "I set them up."

Ophelia blinked a few times. "Oscar, I don't have time to explain. You're going to have to trust me on this." Her (fabulous) face was serious. "It's for the very best reason in the world."

Oscar was about to refuse, but then thought about all the times when Ophelia hadn't trusted the gold buttons he placed on his inventions. They were always for something spectacular. *He* wanted to be trusted, and now Ophelia was asking him to trust *her*. The bubbles in his S.P.I.T. churned with his indecision.

Ophelia threw her paws into the air. "Heat it up like volcano lava *on fire!* Oh, and one more thing—after it's really hot, please wait a few minutes, then hit the fire alarm."

Slowly, Oscar nodded, mentally rehearsing the steps he would need to take to override the FFBI's security system. Determined to summon some stealth (which didn't come naturally to him), Oscar slipped into the FFBI control room and punched in some long codes. Within moments, he'd hacked the system, done a temporary override of the FFBI HQ's temperature, and erased the evidence of his presence on the security cameras. Quickly, the building's heat started to rise. He left the room undetected.

Down the hall, Ophelia made herself inconspicuous and found a paper fan in her special-ops bag. She'd recently pilfered it from a Japanese gallery and was happy to have the chance to try it out. While she cooled herself beside an air vent, she watched as everyone in the FFBI competition gallery began complaining and shedding their extra clothing layers.

Oscar approached her. "Sure is hot in here!"

"Indeed," Ophelia agreed. "It's purr-fect. *Nice work*. No doubt, it won't be lava-like for long. Milton will have his tech cats on this problem immediately. Please go ahead and hit the fire alarm now. I just need a little chaos and one minute more in here." She heard a random bark and looked over at P.U.G. playing with its robo-friends. "Also, extract the robo-mutt from the remote control day care over there. We'll need to make a rather fast and fur-ious exit."

Her mission complete, Ophelia left the gallery as quickly as she had entered.

When she emerged downstairs, Ophelia realized she was clutching the action figure so tightly that she'd left claw puncture marks.

She'd missed it so much! And even with its new

unibrow (thanks to Pierre's very bad customization ideas), she was ecstatic. "You're safe with me, Captain Claw-some. And now we've got to go *steal a mew-seum.*"

"They say 'actions speak louder than words.'
But a really good hiss speaks loudest of all."

—Ophelia von Hairball V

17

IT TAKES A
(FURRY & FINNED) VILLAGE

O scar drove as Ophelia made phone calls. With efficiency and confidence, she spoke to several different cat allies in Amsterdam.

"I know it seems like a strange request, but I'm going to call in a few favors today," Ophelia purred to Natalie, a very connected FFBI agent. "If you don't mind assembling a skilled crew, I need the best of the best. I'm an hour and a half from the city, and I'm in a bit of a hurry."

"Moving mountains today, Ophelia?" Natalie asked.

"Better." Ophelia giggled. "Moving a mewseum. But it's a very small one."

"Leave it to me," Natalie assured her. "They don't call me the miracle mew-ver and shaker for nothing. By the time you're here, your crew will be ready."

"You sure know a lot of cats." Oscar was impressed.

"It's not enough to know them," Ophelia told him. "Wherever you go and whatever you do, make sure when you build connections that you're also building good relationships."

"That's kind of tough for me," Oscar admitted. "I'm a little shy."

"When you're feeling shy, put your dramatic skills to good use." Ophelia put her paw out the window and let the wind move it up and down like a wave. "Believe it or not, even I used to be scared of many new things. But I practiced being brave. After enough practice, one day you'll just *feel* brave." She grinned at him. "In other words, fish—fake it till you make it!"

"You're the bravest, snazziest cat I know." Oscar glanced at her with admiration.

"Why, thank you. And you're the smartest, most innovative inventor I know." She put her sunglasses on. "Now, enough with this sentimental fluff. We've got only a couple of hours to pull this off and get back to Brussels. Let me take you through the plan. It won't be easy and will require impeccable timing."

Ophelia consulted her (old-fashioned) map. "Almost there. Turn right on the next street."

Oscar slowed the car. He reached out and tapped twice on their car's high-tech dashboard. A screen popped up. "Tap the second gold button to the left."

"What's that one for?" Ophelia asked, still a bit unsure about the mysterious and powerful gold buttons Oscar always put on his inventions.

"Detection. It has some personalized touches and detects one thousand and seventeen important things: dogs, inventors, chocolate fountains,

X-Files, karaoke establishments, bass players, libraries—"

Ophelia cut him off with the wave of a paw. They didn't have time. "Let's do this!" She tapped the button.

A little avatar of P.U.G. showed up on-screen and played an audio alert. "Good day, Ophelia. Please be aware there is heavy CCIA presence in the area. There are two water fountains in the vicinity and a thirty percent chance of rain. As well, there is an exclusive hat shop, a top-rated gelato store, and a civilian on a bench with flatulence in abundance."

"Seriously, Oscar? A P.U.G. alert system?"

The fish laughed. "It's customized, with you in mind. I was simply trying to be thorough! The P.U.G. alert mentioned CCIA presence. Just to be safe, let's do stealth mode?"

"Yes! If there's one thing you need to learn as a valuable sidekick, it is to always try to be two pounces ahead. The CCIA has mutts everywhere. If I were them, after we showed up at the shipwreck site, I'd have made sure that every mew-seum and gallery nearby—big and small—had CCIA surveillance. Thug and I seem to think alike," she admitted.

Oscar took a deep breath and tried to remain calm. "Okay." He tapped the glass of his S.P.I.T. "To stay ahead, we need amazing disguises and stealth moves!"

"Excellent deduction, my dear Wat-fin," Ophelia told him. "What disguises do we have on hand?"

Oscar laughed. "Anything your snazzy heart desires."

The trio picked a few fancy outfits so they could move undetected from the O.M.G. to the mew-seum. Then Oscar put the car into super-

boring mode so it wouldn't attract attention. He parked and locked it. "Will we be driving back to FFBI HQ?"

"No. Please pay for longer-term parking," Ophelia advised. "We'll be leaving by other means. We'll come back for the O.M.G. later."

Oscar sprayed all of them with anti-cat scent, and they sauntered down the block, undetected by a pack of CCIA operatives.

A chopper hovered overhead. "Helicopter wind is fabulous for fur fluffiness," Ophelia mentioned to Oscar as they climbed to the roof of the tiny mew-seum. From the helicopter above, a crew descended, then dropped ropes with large hooks.

Ophelia surveyed the scene below her. The tiny mew-seum was totally unplugged from the earth, and everyone had left the building. "Are the hooks going to hold?" Ophelia asked over the helicopter noise. "Even if there's wind?"

"I'm not a fan of hooks," Oscar retorted, inspecting each one, "but these will hold. Have faith in your fish!"

Ophelia spotted a small aircraft closing in.

It had the CCIA symbol on the side. *Those dogs are never far behind!*

"We're secure!" Oscar confirmed. Ophelia nodded, looked up to the FFBI pilot, and gave the claws-up signal. She skillfully lowered ropes and harnesses. Oscar, Ophelia, and P.U.G. were quickly pulled up into the chopper. In a flash, with the mew-seum firmly attached, they were high above Amsterdam, quickly flying away from the CCIA aircraft.

"Call ahead to FFBI HQ security," Ophelia said. "The CCIA will follow us there and attempt to get this mew-seum back. The HQ roof is massive and will easily fit this little building, but we'll need the FFBI building and rooftop secured. Those dogs will try to make a woof-top arrest."

"You think of everything," Oscar sighed with awe.

Meow.

"I came, I clawed, I conquered."

—Ophelia von Hairball V

18

THE TIME IS MEOW

They landed on the helipad of the FFBI HQ with only minutes to spare. Above them, the CCIA circled, but the FFBI security dome would easily hold them off. Ophelia gave a little wave to Thug. He respectfully tipped his hat to her.

"Are we going to make it in time?" Oscar puffed, and hopped out. "According to my very precise timepiece, we have only fifty-seven seconds to get back inside to the competition! Follow us, P.U.G.!"

They ran inside and saw a crowd in front of the elevator. "Use the stairs!" Ophelia shouted. "We have to get to the gallery before they lock the doors!"

The trio raced down from the rooftop. Just before the M.E.O.W. competition timer went off and the doors were locked, they entered. Pierre rolled his eyes when he saw them.

Ophelia and Oscar were breathing heavily. Before they joined the larger crowd, Ophelia stopped at their pedestal and dropped her special-ops bag.

Dressed to the nines, Director MEW took the

podium at the front of the room. "Welcome, elite cat burglars." Applause broke out. "All treasures must be in this room now. I will be moving through the gallery and examining each of them. There will, of course, be only one winner. But we are a great and mighty team. Not only am I so proud of all your burglary skills, I am proud of your team-work." Ophelia couldn't be sure, but she thought MEW looked directly at her.

Ophelia and Oscar followed the crowd around the room as Director MEW examined each stolen offering. When she got to Pierre and Norman's display, Pierre stood tall. "This, Director MEW, is a great moment for me." Norman stuck his tongue out and knocked on the pedestal for attention. "Um…knock-knock! Hello. What about *this* frog?"

"Oh, right," Pierre corrected. "It's a great mo-ment *for me and Norman*." He grinned and pulled off the red blanket that covered their treasure. "We are so excited to reveal this masterpiece!"

MEW gasped, then smiled with delight. "*Cats Playing Cards*? It's not a myth! It wasn't lost! This is a *legendary* find!" she exclaimed. "And it's

uncanny! We were going to set up a special FFBI competition to find this very painting!" With her excitement, the whole room erupted with applause and murmurs; all the cats were impressed with the loot. Everyone's eyes moved tensely between Pierre and Ophelia. *Could it be that Pierre had finally beat his cousin?*

The authenticator briefly examined the painting and did a scan of it. "Of course, I'll have to take this to my lab. But as far as I can tell, this paint compound matches the era it was painted in. And the brushstrokes seem consistent with Catius Clawridge's work."

MEW turned to Ophelia and Norman. "Well, you two. I'm not sure what you have for us, but Pierre and Norman may have outdone you this time. If I may say so, I am enjoying the family rivalry. I think it's making both you and Pierre into better burglars."

A sharp surge of anger jolted through Ophelia, and the fur stood up on her neck. She looked at her smug, cheating cousin and his smarmy frog inventor.

MEW's epic whiskers twitched with confusion. Norman stuck out his tongue. "Go ahead, test it."

Oscar piped up. As he spoke, he stared into Norman's eyes. "It will test as real because they've used canvas from that painting's era and perhaps even scraped paint to reuse from Catius Clawridge's private collection. Check the news. I bet there are reports of stolen Clawridge works. Paint compounds can be re-created!"

Pierre's unibrow furrowed, and his eyes narrowed. Surprised chatter started softly in the gallery but quickly rose in volume as the cat burglars speculated about what had actually happened. Pierre hissed and stopped forward. MEW put her paw up to silence him, but Pierre ignored her.

The entire group of cat burglars followed MEW
upstairs. When she'd unlocked the area, everyone
pounced to see what Ophelia and Oscar had to
show. There were gasps when they saw the mew-
seum sitting there.

"We can walk in," Ophelia assured Director

MEW. "It's all stable." She turned to the FFBI authenticator. "If you put your scanner on the floor in the main room, you'll see that this mew-seum itself is the original home of *Cats Playing Cards*." Ophelia handed MEW several documents. "There are mentions of the painting's location on the floor documented in several different publications. I've been gathering proof for years. The painting under this mew-seum's floor is the real deal."

MEW whispered to the official FFBI authenticator, who nodded. "Everyone back inside!"

Director MEW delivered a blow that shook Oscar to his finned core. "I'm afraid not. The rules state that the stolen items had to be in this room by the time the competition ended. Unfortunately, while you've *no doubt* found the most valuable item, it's not in the gallery. So your mew-seum on the roof doesn't count." She patted Oscar's shoulder and moved on to evaluate the rest of the work. "Now, if you'll excuse me, I've got a few more treasures to examine."

Oscar sank to the floor, beside himself with grief. "My first competition ends in defeat!"

"Some say I'm bossy. Of course, what they mean is that I'm strong, smart, confident, and fabulous—that is to say, *I'm a boss.*"

—Ophelia von Hairball V

19

SUR-PURR-IZE!

Oscar and Ophelia sat together against the wall. Oscar put his head on Ophelia's shoulder. "I'm so sorry I let you down. I'm usually so precise! I should have remembered the rules!"

"No worries, fish! We had quite an adventure, though, didn't we? And my car! I love how the O.M.G. purrs along the road. That's a win! Plus, you got me to go into the sea. No small feat."

"Yes," he sniffled, his S.P.I.T. fogging up. "Adventures are nice. And I'm glad you like the new car. But you just *LOST YOUR TITLE* as the world's number one cat burglar."

Confused, Oscar blinked tears from his bulgy eyes, pulled himself up, and followed Ophelia. Director MEW and the authenticator had finished their rounds and were heading up to the podium to announce the official winner of the M.E.O.W. competition.

"Excuse me, Director MEW!" Ophelia exclaimed. "Before you make a final decision, I think you may have forgotten to look at the Team O² entry. Oscar and I do have a treasure in this room we want considered."

"You relinquished the Amewthyst Scepter!" MEW said.

"Yes." Ophelia nodded.

"And you agree that the mew-seum on the roof doesn't count?"

"We totally understand that," Ophelia said.

"Then what is your submission?" MEW asked.

Ophelia reached into her special-ops bag and took out Captain Claw-some. "This!" she exclaimed boldly. She placed her beloved action figure on the pedestal.

Pierre jumped out of the crowd to confront her. His furious face was close to hers, and his words were angry sputters. "What? When?! HOW DID THIS HAPPEN?"

"Easy," Ophelia said calmly, and stared him down until he took a step back. "I stole it back from you, dear cousin, earlier today when you took off your jacket." She turned to MEW. "It is a legitimate entry. It fulfills all the FFBI competition requirements. Oscar and I pilfered it together, and it was in this room before the doors were locked. The Captain Claw-some action figure is our M.E.O.W. competition official entry!"

Director MEW forced a smile and shook her head. "I'm so sorry, you two. While an old action figure certainly holds sentimental value, I don't think I have to tell you that it's *not* the most valuable thing in this room. Instead, Gemma and her teammate, Andrew, take the cake with their first-edition copy of the book *The Canterpurry Tales*."

"Lovely find." Ophelia acknowledged Gemma and Andrew with a bow. "But if you'll just give me a moment, Director MEW, I'll show you that this action figure holds much, much more than sentimental value." The entire room was silent. All eyes were on Ophelia as she took the action figure and lifted up its tattered, worn shirt. There was a small screw on its back.

"Oh, Oscar—dear and valuable sidekick and team member, will you please hand me a tiny screwdriver?"

"At your service," Oscar replied, his beating heart and fast breathing creating waves in his S.P.I.T. He pulled out a screwdriver and passed it to the cat.

With care, Ophelia opened a minuscule panel on the back of Captain Claw-some. Inside was a tattered, rolled, old paper. Her voice was a quiet, confident purr. "*This* is what we are entering to win the M.E.O.W. competition!"

"What is it?"

Ophelia spoke softly, but her tone commanded the attention of everyone in the room. "It is the only map *in the entire world* that shows how to find the long-lost city of Catlantis. My grandmother sealed it away in this figure before she passed on. I

haven't seen this since I was just a small fluff-ball."

Pierre and Norman both hunched over, their mouths gaping open with shock. Oscar couldn't help himself and, with glee, he released the single fly he'd been carrying with him for a special occasion like this. The bug flew right toward Norman and into his open mouth. Terrified and disgusted, the frog ran out of the room. Pierre had no words, but his wrinkled unibrow displayed his fury.

"Cats off to you, Ophelia and Oscar. Indeed, that map is beyond priceless. What a memorable day!" Director MEW moved up behind the podium. "Not only have Ophelia von Hairball V and her inventor, Oscar Fishgerald Gold, won this competition, but they've also been awarded the prestigious DreamTeam Award!"

The excited bubbles in Oscar's S.P.I.T. made it almost impossible for Ophelia to see his eyes, but she thought she caught a glimpse of happy tears. Unable to help herself, Ophelia hugged Oscar with all her might.

"Don't push your luck, fish-face." Ophelia winked at her sidekick. Together, they accepted their award.

"Speech! Speech!" the other cats called.

"I only really have one thing to say," Ophelia told the crowd. "If you believe in what you're doing and the why behind it, unexpected and great things will happen. In you is the power to overcome obstacles and pounce on your dreams."

Oscar spoke, too. "And don't forget that

teamwork really does make the dream work."

Then Ophelia von Hairball V of Burglaria and her scaly senior inventor, Oscar Fishgerald Gold, posed (fabulously) for all the photos.

"We look exceptionally fin-tastic," Oscar declared.

"Purr-fect, un-fur-gettable, and claw-some," she agreed.

EPILOGUE

FFBI CAT BURGLAR TIP: Life is short. Work hard for what you believe. Sparkle bright at every opportunity. And remember, there is always someone in the world who wants to be on your team. (They're probably not dogs.)

ACKNOWLEDGMENTS

Super-sparkle gratitude to Gemma Cooper of the Bent Agency and to Erin Stein, Nicole Otto, Weslie Turner, Natalie C. Sousa, and every single person on Macmillan's Imprint team who helped Snazzy Cat Capers come to life. Also thanks to some very, very special people in our lives who have, at one time or another, helped us to understand the powerful things that can happen when you mix creativity, teamwork, and some indestructible rose-colored glasses.

ABOUT THE AUTHOR & ILLUSTRATOR

DEANNA KENT and **NEIL HOOSON** have worked on books, brand and marketing campaigns, and interactive experiences. Deanna loves twinkle string lights, black licorice, and Edna Mode, and she may be the only person on the planet who says "teamwork makes the dream work" without a hint of sarcasm. Neil is king of a Les Paul guitar, makes killer enchiladas, and really wants aliens to land in his backyard. By far, their greatest creative challenge is raising four (very busy, very amazing) boys. Snazzy Cat Capers is their first chapter book series.

#1 DREAMTEAM

TREASURE HUNTING LAWS

TUNNEL TIPS

#1

ODDS & ENDS